W9-BXR-571

Fountaindale
Public Library

300 W. Briarcliff Road
Bolingbrook, Illinois
60439

Hester

by
Byron Barton

GREENWILLOW BOOKS

A Division of William Morrow & Company, Inc./New York

Copyright © 1975 by Byron Barton. All rights reserved. No part of this book may be reproduced without permission from the Publisher, Greenwillow Books, 105 Madison Ave., New York, N.Y. 10016.
Printed in the United States of America.   4   5

Library of Congress Cataloging in Publication Data   Barton, Byron. Hester.   [1. Halloween—Fiction]
I. Title.   PZ7.B2848He   [E]   75-9668   ISBN 0-688-80009-2   ISBN 0-688-84009-4 lib. bdg.

Fountaindale Public Library District
300 West Briarcliff Road
Bolingbrook, Illinois 60439
(312) 759-2102

Hester was
dressed early for
her Halloween party.
While she waited for
her friends to arrive,
she decided to go out

to all of her neighbors for trick-or-treats.

But she soon decided that she would look

for a more unusual place to spook.

I'll try this house, Hester thought.

She went up to the door and rang the bell.

An old lady answered and Hester yelled,

"TRICK-OR-TREAT!"

The lady smiled.

"Come in, my dear."

"These are my friends,"
the lady said.
"Won't you join us?"

Hester was polite. "Hello," she said.

"This is a very nice house you live in."

"Thank you," said the old lady. "You're very kind.

Would you like to see more?"

The lady showed Hester the rest of the house.

"This is my favorite room," she said.

"And these are my favorite clothes

and my favorite hat

and my favorite broom. Would you like to go for a ride?"

With the old lady up front and Hester behind,

they went flying into the night.

High above the buildings, the two of them flew.

Then they came back, but a little too fast and

CRASH !!

The broom was broken into bits.

"Here, take mine," Hester said. "Thank you, my dear," said the old lady.

Then Hester said good-by and hoped she would see them all again next year.

Hester hurried home to her party.

When Hester got home, her mother wondered what happened to her broom.

But before Hester could explain, her friends began to arrive.

And they all had a wonderful time.